THE BIG ADVENTURE
OF A LITTLE LINE

Serge Bloch

THE BIG ADVENTURE
OF A LITTLE LINE

Thames & Hudson

I was out walking one day when I saw it.
A little line, lying by the side of the road.

I picked it up and took a closer look.
Sitting on the palm of my hand,
it didn't look like much.
Just a tiny little bit of a line.

I put it safely in my pocket
and took it home.

I kept it on a shelf with my other treasures,
between a snail shell and a pretty pebble.

And then I forgot about it...
at least for a while.

But from time to time, I thought about it.

One day, I took it down from the shelf
and put it on an open page in my notebook.
It moved, just a little.

"Come on, you can do it!" I said.
It moved again.

I think it wanted to draw something.
Finally, it made a wobbly sort of circle
that looked a bit like a potato.

Then it curled up and fell asleep.
It must have been tired.

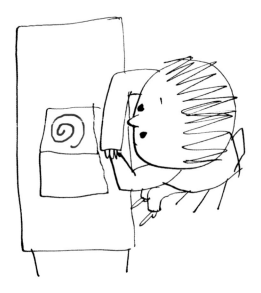

I began to open up my notebook
every day, just to talk to it.

It looked up at me and wriggled.
I think it wanted to play.

Little by little, we got to know each other.

At first, I taught it to turn into simple things.
A hat, a bike, a ball.

Then it drew more complicated things.
My line was pretty clever.

We became inseparable.

We wandered through life together.

When I was scared, it quivered.

But it always protected me.

Sometimes we would sit beside each other.
It would stretch out and draw the horizon.
If you looked very carefully,
you could even see a ship in the distance.

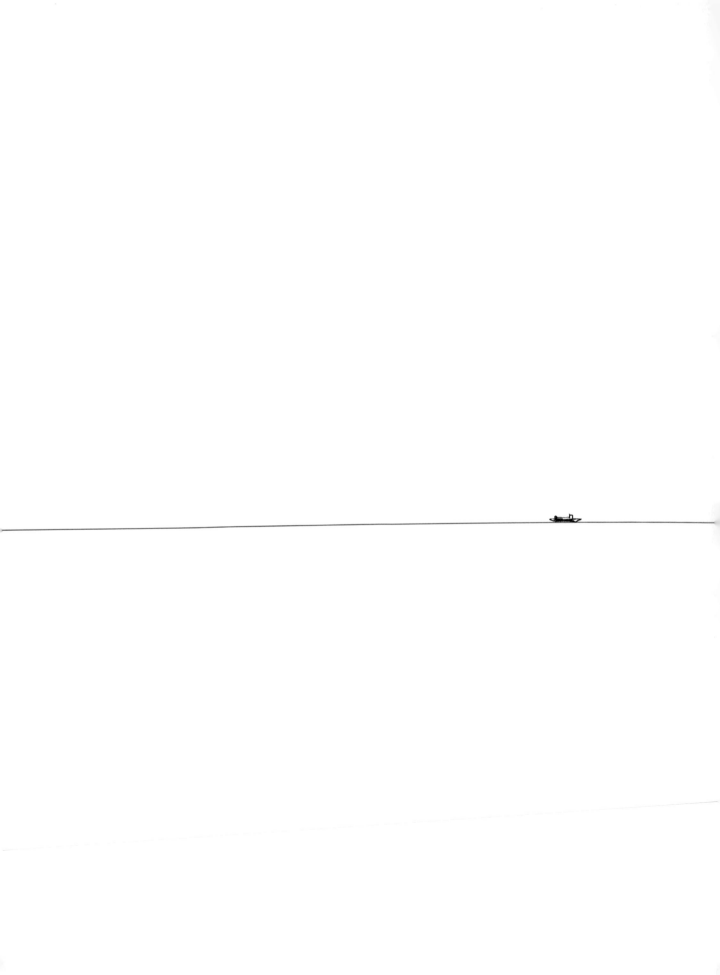

I grew up.
My line grew up too.

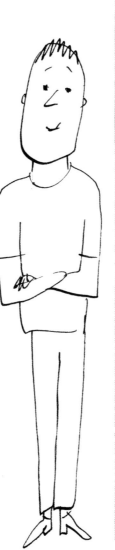

The line wasn't always easy to live with.
It could make me see red, or give me the blues.

Sometimes it wouldn't do what I wanted.
It scrawled and squealed and drove me crazy.

Sometimes it liked to hide from me.
I hunted everywhere for it.

But it always turned up again.

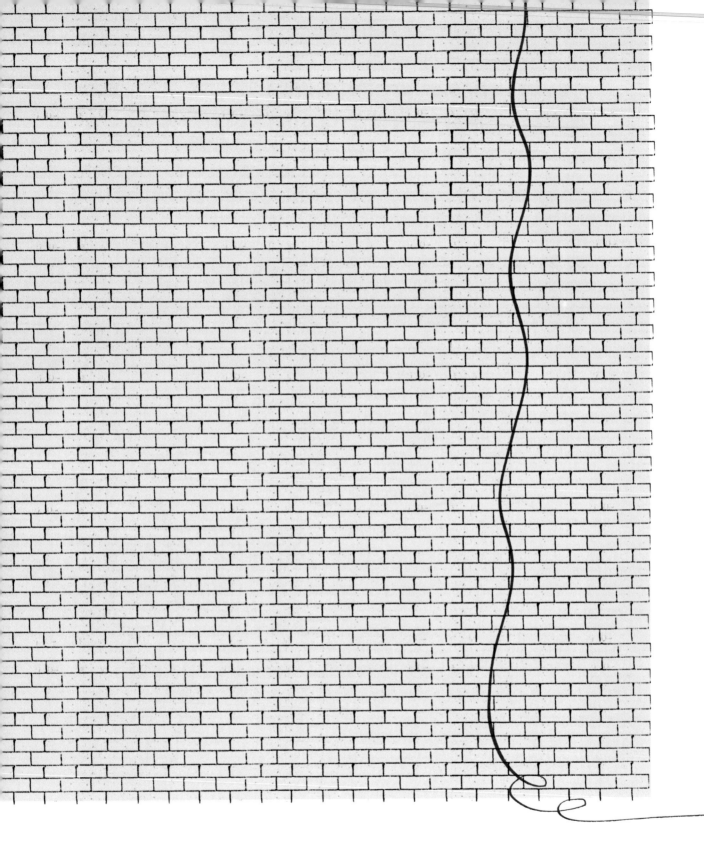

Then we ran away together...

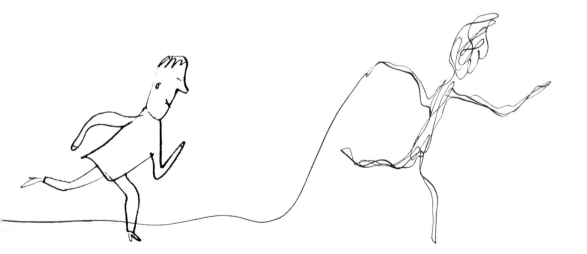

... and I felt like I could fly!

Everything seemed easy.
We made children smile.

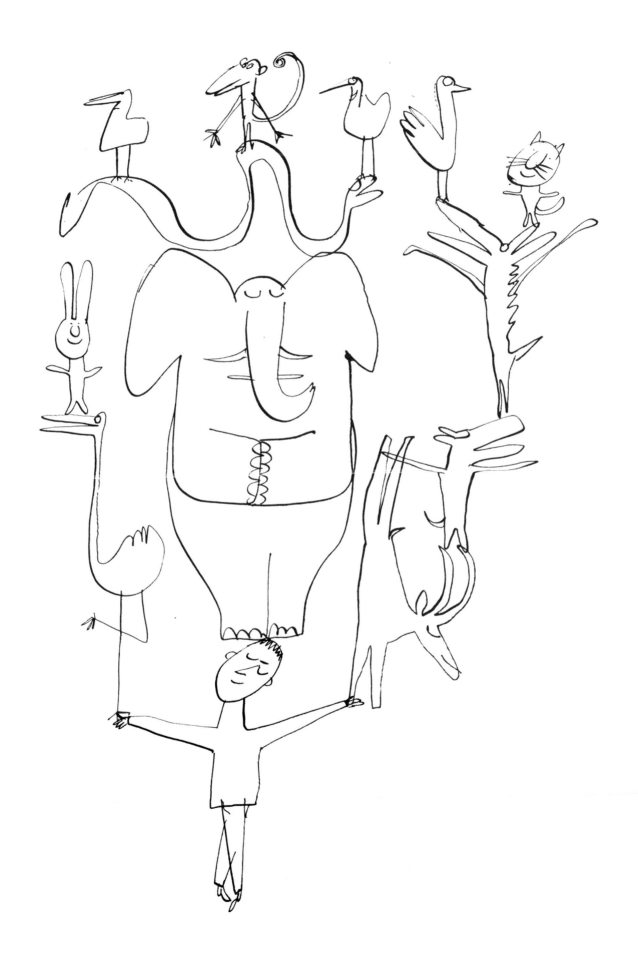

We told stories and made people laugh...

...and made them cry too.

We did dangerous things together...

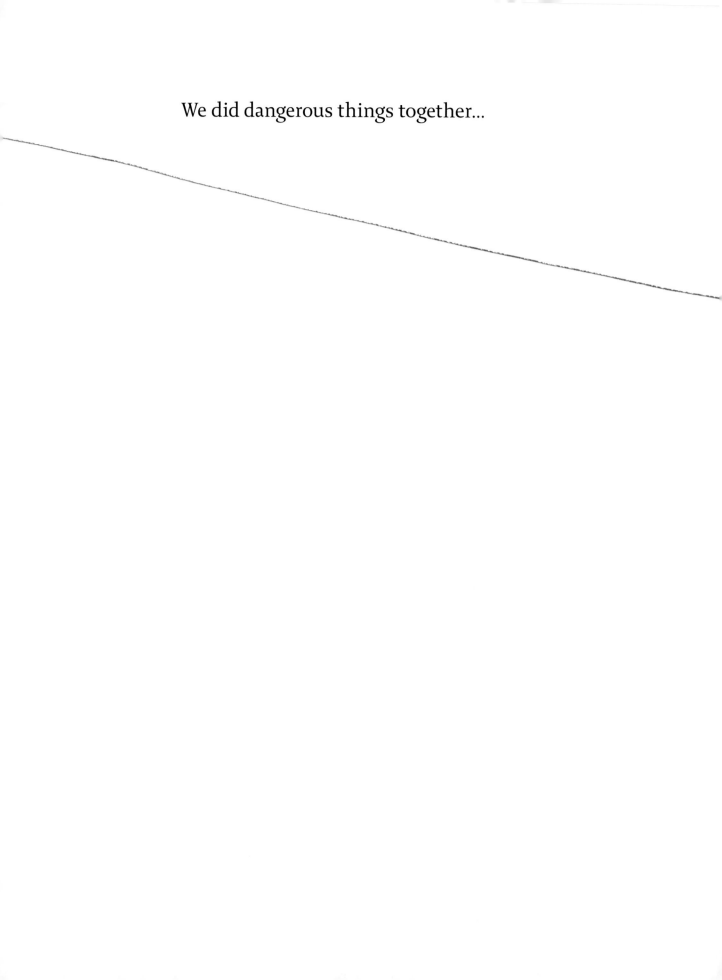

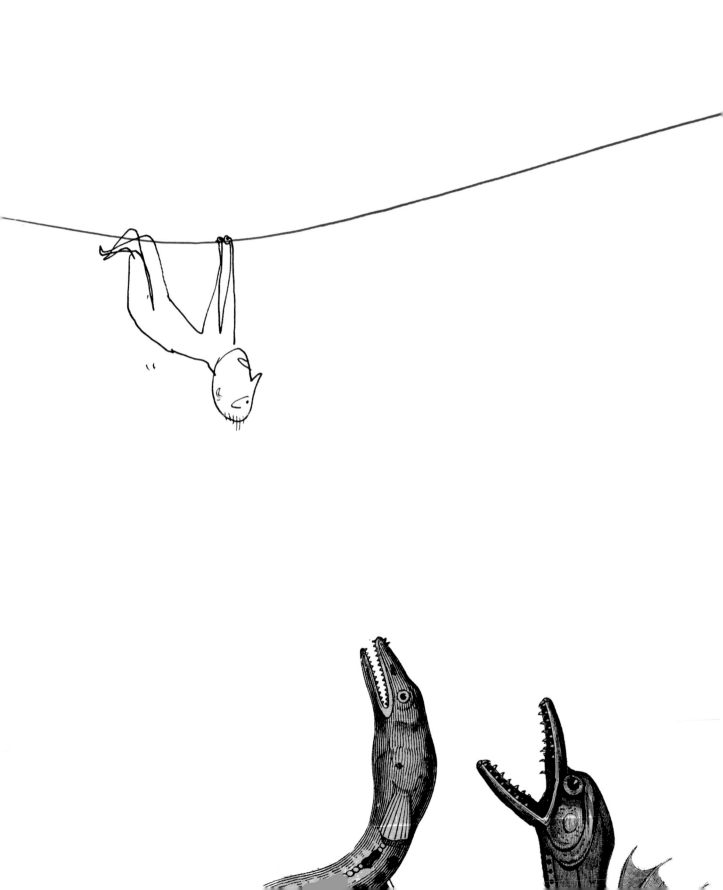

...but it always worked out in the end!

My line and I went around the world together.

We went to art exhibitions.

We met famous people.

Life was magical!

Then time passed by...

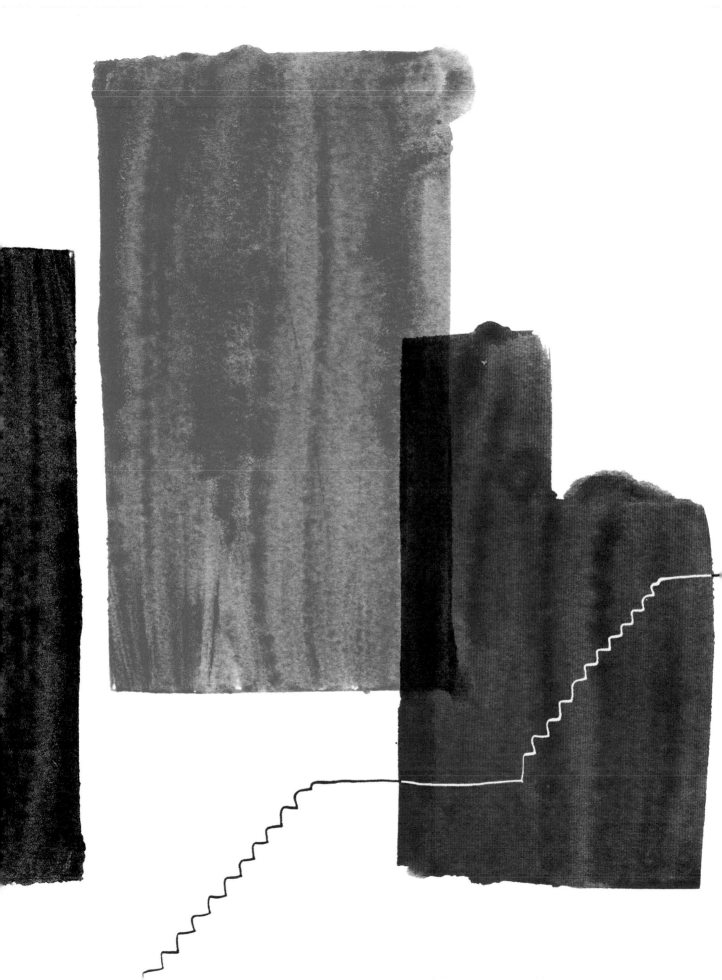

Sometimes quietly...

Sometimes quickly...

Sometimes sadly.

One day, I decided that the time had come.
And the line agreed with me.

So I cut off a piece of the line,
just a tiny little bit.

And then…

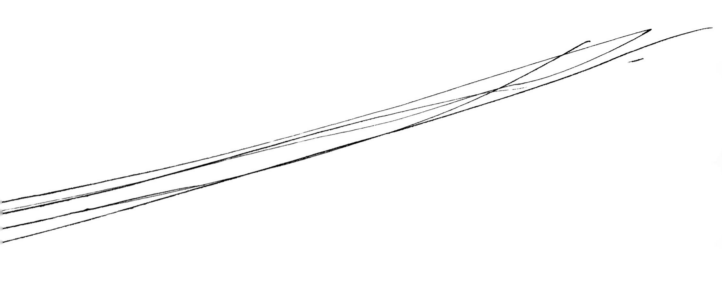

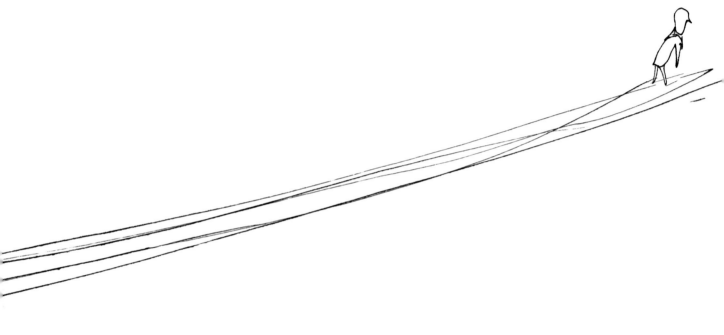

for:

Charles Addams
Saul Bass
Martin Berthommier
Jean-Louis Besson
Guy Billout
Quentin Blake
R .O. Blechman
Jean Bosc
Alexander Calder
Chaval
Seymour Chwast
André François
André Franquin
Yves Got
Michel Granger
George Herriman
Philippe Kailhenn
Paul Klee
Lionel Koechlin
Pascal Lemaitre
El Lissitzky
Maryan
Joan Miró
René Pétillon
Philippe Petit-Roulet
Paul Rand
Jean-Marc Reiser
Maurice Rosy
Raymond Savignac
Ronald Searle
Jean-Jacques Sempé
Ben Shahn
Shel Silverstein
Siné
Ralph Steadman
William Steig
Saul Steinberg
Roland Topor
Tomi Ungerer
Georges Wolinski
and all the others...

The author and publisher would like to thank
the Conseil Général du Val-de-Marne for
their invaluable support for this project.

Translated from the French *La grande histoire d'un petit trait*

First published in the United Kingdom in 2015 by
Thames & Hudson Ltd, 181A High Holborn, London WC1V 7QX

www.thamesandhudson.com

First published in 2015 in hardcover in the United States of America by
Thames & Hudson Inc., 500 Fifth Avenue, New York, New York 10110

thamesandhudsonusa.com

Original edition © 2014 Éditions Sarbacane, Paris
This edition © 2015 Thames & Hudson Ltd, London

British Library Cataloguing-in-Publication Data
A catalogue record for this book is available from the British Library

Library of Congress Catalog Card Number 2015937878

ISBN 978-0-500-65058-5

Printed in Malaysia